CARRY-ON

RAMONA SAPPHIRE

authorHOUSE®

AuthorHouse™
1663 Liberty Drive
Bloomington, IN 47403
www.authorhouse.com
Phone: 1 (800) 839-8640

Published by AuthorHouse 01/17/2017

ISBN: 978-1-5246-5814-4 (sc)
ISBN: 978-1-5246-5813-7 (e)

Print information available on the last page.

This book is printed on acid-free paper.

Author's Note

Thanks so much for selecting my publication for your reading pleasure. I enjoy writing stories on assorted topics based on experience and overall -- imagination. I'll admit I'm a bit eccentric and quirky. Many of my stories may comprise an element of inspiration, are outrageous, raunchy, mysterious, bizarre, insightful, or even simple, to say the least. And most recently, cringe humor and spoof writing has been added to my repertoire of genres.

A very special thanks to those who believed in me, inspired, pushed, and supported me, and appreciated my own distinct style of story-telling rather comparing me to others.

Very special thanks to the well-meaning critics that compelled the necessary *expedient* changes. Your expertise has been far-reaching and helpful, for which I am eternally grateful.

Foremost, are my thanks to God via the gift of breath and hence the wit, imagination, strength, and courage to inspire others and to keep dreaming and pushing.

And lastly, supreme thanks to mommy for her never-failing positive, "It's nice to be nice," attitude and undying encouragement and support.

Prologue

"Look, I can explain, p-p-please don't shoot!"

Kenna was livid and pointing the revolver dead at her husband, James' head. He was one clip short of getting blown away.

"It's not what it looks like, I swear!"

"Kick rocks, heifer! Kenna spewed at Molly, cocking the revolver.

"Please, just listen!" said James. L-let me tell you what hap..."

"Did I stutter? I said shut up Bobble Head before I pull this trigger!"

***

Ulyssa was floored. The red carry-on bag she held was buzzing. She'd just returned to her apartment from her flight. Her gaze swiveled between her cell phone and the bag. Was she trippin'? How could this be?

***

BAM! Calvin was hit so hard, his torso ejected like toast from a toaster and body-slammed against the street pavement. Spectators surrounded the victim like ants. There were numerous cell phones sneak-snapping amid cries of "Oh shit!" "Did you see that?" "Is he dead?"

The taxi driver scurried out of the cab to his side. "Oh lawd! What have I done to this poor fella? Why'd he run out in front of me like that? Are you okay?"

A set of heels galloped toward the direction of the accident. Claudia was mortified at what she'd just witnessed. Well, so much for having my way with him," Claudia mumbled, coyly.

Chapter 1

In the twilight of nightfall, the gargantuan passenger aircraft glided through the vaporized billowy clouds. The roar of its engines approached the landing amid twinkling townships, winding roads, and bodies of water that'd earlier resembled a Monopoly board from the skytop...

"Hand me that bag overhead, would you?" insisted Miss Lora of the airline attendant, begrudgingly.

"Which one's yours, ma'am?" the attendant asked, obliging her reluctantly.

Ulyssa, the flight attendant, reached up to the carry-on bag compartment displaying a perfectly round-shaped rump and ample cleavage to the pleasure of Felix seated nearby. He was ogling her unabashedly.

"The red one," grumbled Ms. Lora. "Ole nasty dog," she muttered, eying Felix zooming in on the flight attendant's derrière.

Crinkly eyed and despondent, the silver-haired elder was slumped in her seat in the aircraft. She was purportedly consumed by ailments that debilitated her. Over time she'd reportedly developed a weak heart, slight dowager's hump, and severed nerve endings that caused tingling in her upper and lower extremities and excruciating pain. Supposedly attributed to this, she was considerably grumpy and rude.

Ulyssa, a long-legged, scrumptious dashing redhead, could sense her admirer's lewd eyes burning through his sockets. She retrieved the first red carry-on on sight in a huff and lugged it down.

Next, salt and pepper-haired Felix, about mid-fifties, fetched the remaining carry-on from the compartment that was also red. He was in a hurry and purportedly failed to examine it, his eyes so fixated on Ulyssa. He then scurried from the front of the plane and exited.

***

The sky was salmon-pink, turquoise, royal-purple, and gold-tinged. The stoic cornstalks waned like soldiers in the infinite winding creek-containing heavily forested fields. This showcased in the windows throughout the interstate bus ride.

The pristine white pinwheel-like wind turbines prevailed in farmlands of silver domes, farmhouses, farm animals, and miniscule townships. This subsequently evolved into the incorrigible nightlife of the city, as it was known by its denizens. The bus finally crawled into the station…

"Let me help you with that," insisted Horwood.

Kenna, scrunching her nose and nauseated from his funk, stuttered and said, "Th-that's all right, I got this."

"No, I got it," he said, lifting it kindly from her hands and flinging it into the carry-on compartment.

A luscious-looking blond-black-streak-haired woman and her two school-aged children had boarded the bus homeward-bound. After they'd settled in, mom seized her carry-on and struggled to stuff it into the overhead compartment. Witnessing her struggles, Horwood had rushed to her aid.

Kenna had complied, held her nose, and politely thanked him, barely acknowledging him. She hurriedly resettled herself in her seat beside her kids.

***

The synchronous rattle of the train serenaded its passengers as it coasted along the tracks to the station. Along the way, the expansive windows boasted picturesque landscapes of ubiquitous townships. These contained warehouses, storefronts, worship places, skyscrapers and more. Apparent were patches of pedestrians milling about randomly beneath the golden-orange, bluish, purplish, dusky canopy of sky…

"Excuse me," said Calvin, a passenger on the train. "I need to place my carry-on in the luggage compartment."

"Me too," said Claudia. "Would you mind giving me a hand and sticking mine in there too?"

"Sure," Calvin responded, relieved to get a break from her motor mouth. And he shoved the carry-ons into the luggage compartment, both of which so happened to be red.

A middle-aged balding man named Calvin had earlier boarded the train to Manhattan. He'd vacated his hometown in hopes of a new life. He'd quit his job for higher pay and a lavish lifestyle and what not.

Claudia, rather eccentric and annoying, had bullseyed on Calvin sitting alone on the train and decided to join him. She was quite the Chatty Cathy, or shall we say Chatty Claudia, which annoyed him to the hilt. She was purported to be brilliant and well-educated by her conversation.

Claudia went on and on about her credentials and herself to Calvin's chagrin. He prayed at that point for hearing loss in order to rescue himself from her loose lips. If only he knew.

Calvin visualized Claudia's large full oversized lips, red as roses, yakking and yakking galore. The more she yakked, the fuller and larger they swelled and multiplied. He dozed off intermittently unbeknownst to her. The echo of her yakking was maddening to him.

When the train finally pulled into the station, it was nightfall. Calvin retrieved the first red carry-on bag he beheld and high-tailed it out of there like a bat out of hell, leaving a trail of Claudia's "It's been nice talking to you..." in his wake.

Chapter 2

Kenna was quite a handful and a drama queen. She was known for blowing everything out of proportion. Despite this, seemingly, her husband, James loved her dearly. He'd put up with all her nonsense and all the baggage she was carrying from past wounds.

After all, James a rather short, thick, and average Kevin-Hart-looking kinda guy, but a sweetheart, wasn't unflawed himself. He had some issues and wounding likewise. However, he purportedly kept his stuff under wraps.

James and Kenna met at a house party of a mutual friend and seemed to hit it off right away. They'd dated some time, however not without incident. Years later, they'd decided to get married. Kenna was thrilled to finally have a responsible man to look after her and her two kids, and she truly loved James with all her heart, so it seemed.

You see, Kenna's kids were not her husband's. But she was beautiful and a responsible mom with a good heart; she meant well. However, every now and then there was some baby daddy drama going on with the kids between Kenna and their dad, Nathaniel, Nate for short. And James would put up with their derelict father to a limit. However, when Nate would badger his wife to the point of jeopardizing their marriage, that was a deal breaker for him. He wasn't having that mess and he'd wind up cussing out Nate and cutting off his visitation.

Things would be copesthetic for a minute until the kids would scream for daddy and misbehave with him. Then he'd acquiesce and beg Kenna to take them to their dad. However, the problem was that Nate lived with his mom and oftentimes grandma didn't care to be bothered. Besides the kids eating her out of house and home, Nate's broke ass could never afford to take his kids anywhere, so he'd wind up overstaying his welcome visiting them at Kenna and James' place.

Kenna was traveling the bus home that evening and returning from her family reunion at her cousin's house down south. They had a real farm with pigs and chickens and everything. The food was super-delicious and fresh. She and the kids always enjoyed their visits with Deacon Joe, Cousins Mae-Mae, June Bug, Uncle Frankie, Uncle Moonie, Ms. Dolly, Uncle Scrappy, Sister Sally, Pookie, and the rest of the family.

Kenna was surveying her messages on her cell phone as usual when these peculiar texts surfaced. They appeared to be for another woman named Molly, and misdirected to her phone.

"What the? Who the hell is this Molly?" Kenna whispered, scanning the multiple text messages.

Next she blew up and screamed, "Oh hell no!" as the messages became lewder. No telling what would happen next, she resigned to drop the children at Nate's house despite his caring to be bothered or not!

Kenna continued to read the so-called misdirected text messages growing hotter and hotter by the minute. And to make matters worse, all the messages stemmed from her husband, James. "He's going to pay for cheating on me like this. I've got some tricks up my sleeve too, silly rabbit," she vowed, aloud.

Kenna went on and on, fantasizing about how she was going to divorce her husband and take every penny he had and the house, so she imagined. The kids stared mortified at her expression, but didn't really care, considering "he ain't my daddy" anyway, they'd claim.

Kenna thought about busting James out but decided she'd wait until she got home. He'd only deny it anyway, clueless she had proof from the text messages. She planned to grill him to the max to see how much he'd lie to her face.

Kenna rose from her seat to retrieve her carry-on bag. And that is when Horwood had rushed over to assist her.

As soon as the bus crept into the station, Kenna was the first to eject from her seat and open the luggage compartment. Seeing her frustration in seizing her bag, Horwood immediately rushed over to assist her against her wishes. She politely conceded, holding her nose, as he retrieved the red carry-on. Next, she snatched up her children and belongings and bounced off the bus in a tizzy.

***

Earlier, Horwood had admired Kenna's attractiveness and secretly desired to get to know her. He returned to his seat hopeful, depositing an intense trail of funk in his wake.

Horwood, clearly disillusioned and disappointed, drug his stenchful self off the bus. He glanced around hopeful of at least one final glimpse of Kenna. Needless to say, his hopes were squashed.

During the bus ride Horwood had been tagged Mr. Stanky by passengers. Rotten eggs and sweaty feet had nothing on him. His stenchful bouquet trailed him like a vapor. It somersaulted down the aisle like a tumbleweed. Pitied was the passenger who sat beside him. So stenchful was he that as passengers caught wind of him, they'd pinch their noses or make vomiting overtures and double over. His seat companion was no exception. Thank God this was the last stop.

Imagine even the littlest creepy crawlers skittering underfoot killing over from the stench. By chance their plans to inhabit the passengers had been foiled, so perhaps applause was in order.

Nevertheless, one could only conclude Mr. Stanky was homeless and had been estranged from soap and water for a minute. Fortunately, there were only a few moments left before the bus would meet its destination serenaded by choruses of "Glory hallelujah" and "Thank you, Jesus" of relief whispered by passengers.

Poor Horwood.

Chapter 3

"Man am I glad to be home," sighed Ulyssa, toting her shoulder bag and carry-on from her flight that early evening. And just as she was inserting her key into the door, an uncanny thing happened--her cell phone buzzed! Or at least she thought that's what she heard until she realized it wasn't stemming from her shoulder bag.

Something was buzzing inside the red carry-on Ulyssa was toting that startled her. Let's see, she thought, I'm holding my cell phone and the bag is buzzing. Oh my God, it's a bomb! She tossed it on the ground and immediately hopped away from it.

The buzzing stopped. Ulyssa tiptoed toward it after starring at it approximately five minutes. With her body leaned away from it, she poked it gingerly with her red-manicured finger and then studied the luggage tag. And low and behold that's when the realization hit her that it wasn't hers.

Ulyssa cautiously unzipped the bag and extracted the cell phone. The phone contact was associated with an avatar. "You've got to be kidding!" she exclaimed aloud.

***

Ms. Lora laid in her airbed with her killer bug spray beside her. She swore if she saw another critter, she'd squash it with her bare hands and drown it in her bug spray.

The little ole abandoned shack smooshed between a jumble of grafitied deteriorated properties, was dilapidated and cramped. A long-lost relative had flown Ms. Lora to Alabama to hear her cousin's Last Will and Testament. She prayed she'd return with big money. She'd also cozied up to a friend there.

Ms. Lora's cousin had long ago left her with the keys to her smelly ole place here in Michigan where she formerly lived. Ms. Lora was hoping to inherit enough money to fix the place up like new. However, as it turned out, Cousin Eloise was an avid gambler to her detriment.

Crabby ole Ms. Lora had made it reluctantly home. She'd called a ride-sharing service to pick her up from the airport. She'd paid the driver out of her measly inheritance of two thousand dollars, which she aimed to stretch, and rolled her little red carry-on into the house. Something needed to happen soon or she'd find herself out on her ear in the streets. In the meantime, she'd make the best of it.

The airplane ride had been long and arduous for her. She'd laid her carry-on against the narrow hall closet door. She'd not bothered to check the bag as of yet.

Next, she climbed into her little airbed and rehashed the events of the train ride in her mind. "Ole nasty dog,' she thought, as she zoomed in on Felix. She was reminded of his ogling Ulyssa on the plane. Next she crashed.

***

Felix headed for Ms. Lora's house presuming she had his carry-on since he had hers. Later it'd dawned on him to call his cell phone buried in his carry-on to determine who had it indeed. There was some stuff in there he really needed and he was rather hopeful of regaining it. He'd seen how Ms. Lora feasted on him with her ole crinkly eyes on the plane and cringed. Ole nasty dog, he thought.

Felix presented at Ms. Lora's place. By appearances, one would've thought it was abandoned. I hope the old geezer didn't steal anything from my bag, he thought. Well not to worry. It's not like I couldn't beat her down and shake it out of her, he reasoned. He strolled up to the door and pounded firmly on it.

***

Kenna had disappeared in a huff from the bus. She was livid. "How dare he cheat on me!" she exclaimed. "I'm gonna make his sorry ass pay for that!"

Kenna had felt rather special today up until she saw the text from James to his little hussy he must've sent to her mistakenly. She planned to drop her kids off at her babies' daddy momma's house, as she'd promised on the bus, and secure a can of whoop-ass for James, along the way home, whatever that might look like.

Kenna arrived at her babies' daddy momma's house and smashed the doorbell. She'd eyed a set of heads peeking behind the curtains as she was storming up the driveway.

Kenna laid on the doorbell and nobody answered. "Who do they think they're messing with?" she mumbled. "Not today!" She demanded her kids help her bam on the door while she continued to mash the doorbell. "I know you're in there!" she boomed.

Nate and his mother surrendered and bust open the door. They yawned and stretched, feigning drowsiness.

"Why are you all banging' on the door waking us up like that?" asked Nate.

"You must think I'm slow. I saw you guys peeking out that window and now you're perpetrating like you were sleep." Next she shoved her kids into the house before Nate could protest, and dashed off blowing kisses to them.

Knowing James and the little "hoe" were at the house together now, Kenna was clueless about her plans. She was known for being hyper-dramatic and flying off the handle. She needed to make a plan QUICK!

Kenna while bussing it from her kids, Tequlla's and Sunrise's grandma's house, inadvertently discovered she had the wrong carry-on bag. Dammit to hell! My good makeup and flatirons were in that bag, she thought.

Next she'd opened the switched carry-on and her eyes feasted on something truly amazing. She cheesed and whispered, "Yes! God, you must've felt my pain. You knew just what I needed. Hallelujah! Thank you, Jesus!"

Chapter 4

Horwood retrieved his Lexus he routinely parked nearby after finishing his assignments. Entering his vehicle, he cracked the windows, sprayed himself, and quickly changed into fresher duds all from the bag he kept in his trunk. He'd shower when he got home. "I've got to find a better way to make a living. This really sucks but it pays too well to quit," he mumbled to himself.

Horwood drove toward his posh condominium on Lakeside Street with a spectacular view overlooking the cityscape and lakefront. He pulled into the garage and parked his vehicle. From the parking garage he entered into the elevator and cruised to the eighteenth floor like smooth jazz.

Horwood was living large as a plainclothes detective. He also had his own private detective agency. It was amazing what people would hire him to do and the price they were willing to pay for it.

Horwood wore more disguises than he blinked. He spied on people in the most wretched places. It seems the most popular request of his career was playing a smelly homeless man. And though it was starting to get to him, his love of luxury overruled it.

Horwood entered his immaculate upscale fully furnished man cave and headed straight for the emerald-green-taupe-pale-yellow-tiled shower. Nearby was a matching decor Jacuzzi and steam room.

Speaking of handsome, Horwood cleaned up nicely. He resembled a model and muscle builder with swag. He had thick black wavy hair, was buffed or swole as they say, and had chiseled deliberate facial features. He'd been told he was fine but he wasn't cocky about it. Contrarily, Horwood was purportedly humble and very kind and endearing. It was difficult for him to maintain relationships considering his vigorous work schedule and travel.

Horwood fantasized momentarily about Kenna. He regretted wearing the homeless man getup this evening. He truly desired to step to her but surmised it was inappropriate. He decided to abandon all thoughts of her for the time being.

Besides, Horwood needed to retrieve something from his carry-on before he entered the shower. He opened it and gasped! "What the? On no! I don't believe this!"

***

"I've never seen anybody fly so high in the air like that," commented a spectator who'd just witnessed a pedestrian getting hit by a vehicle. "I hope he's still alive."

Calvin was so busy escaping the loose lips of Claudia that he wasn't paying attention. He'd stepped out into the street with his torso forward and his head in the direction of Claudia behind him.

Calvin didn't care to fall victim to Claudia's loose lips anymore. He was attempting to hail a taxi to take him to the hotel he'd reside at until he got squared away at his new job. In the process, he was struck by the very taxi he was hailing and managed to be still squeezing the red carry-on bag when the ambulance arrived.

Earlier, Claudia had finally caught up to Calvin and towered over him, checking his pulse and determining if he was okay until the ambulance arrived. Calvin's eyes were closed but it was apparent he was still alive by his chest heaving. He was groaning a bit, also.

"Look!" exclaimed a spectator. "He's breathing! Thank God he's alive!" he announced, scanning and informing the other spectators as they continued sneak-snapping with their cell phones.

"Ma'am, you're going to have to step aside unless you're his wife or a relative. You can't climb in here."

"I am."

"Then okay, get in."

Calvin was squirming and writhing, thoroughly upset Claudia was beside him, yet relieved he was not alone. Calming himself somewhat, he realized she'd have to suffice for now.

Calvin lay in the emergency room bed being probed, poked, and prodded all over. Claudia was yakking away, ninety miles a minute as usual.

Calvin was sedated, thus plastered most of the time, so it didn't faze him that much. Claudia noticed the carry-ons were switched and she'd exchanged and retrieved her bag, however not without riffling through his first. She'd uncovered paperwork inside with the name and address of the apartment hotel he'd plan to reside at with all his personal info.

Eventually Calvin was released from the emergency room and he was actually grateful Claudia was there to take him to his hotel. However unbeknownst to him, she had a smorgasbord cooking up her sleeve.

Chapter 5

"It's me, Felix."

"I know."

"I'm surprised you even answered the phone, seeing my face and all."

"I started not too but I think you know you have my bag and that I've got yours."

"Uh, no. You've got it twisted. Actually, your mother has your bag and…"

"My mother? I was adopted and she died a couple of years ago. What are you up to, you creep!"

"Look, calm down. You want your bag don't you?" Next, only the sound of Ulyssa's soft breathing was heard. "Are you still there?" asked Felix.

"Yes, I'm here, and yes I do want my bag. But you still haven't explained why you think Ms. Lora's my mother."

"Well, because there are some baby pictures of you in her bag, so she claims, with the name Ulyssa on the back. Apparently she had a baby named Ulyssa that she gave up for adoption."

"What? Are you a con man? I don't have time for your games!"

"Look, calm down. I'm not joshing you. You'll just have to come here and see them for yourself when you pick up your bag. It turns out I had Ms. Lora's bag, you had mine, and she had yours."

"Well, where is she?"

"She's taking a little nap and she would've been afraid to talk to you anyway, seeing how you would be pissed at her for what she did to you."

"She could be quite right. But if all you say is true, I'm willing to get to know her and let her make amends to me. I have a soft heart like that."

"How kind of you. Now about what time do you think you can make it here?" And Felix passed Ulyssa Ms. Lora's address.

"Don't get your panties in a bunch. I'm on my way now."

"Speaking of panties, what color are you wear...."

CLICK!

Who were you talking to just now? asked Ms. Lora, stirring on her airbed from her nap. SWAT! She annihilated a host of critters skittering across the floor with her swatter and spray.

"Oh, I called Ulyssa—you know, the flight attendant, so she can get her bag."

"Uhn hun. So, did she have any money in it?"

"Do you think I would tell you that, ole biddy?" he teased.

"Of course not. What was I thinking?"

"But to answer your question, there were no valuables. I'm sure she had all that stuff in her shoulder bag, which most of you women carry."

"I'm sure you're right. We'll, I'm up now. How about a cup of tea?"

Felix eyed two more critters skittering across the floor. "No thanks, I'm good—You know, on second thought, sure." If only she knew.

***

James and Molly were in place on the sofa relaxing and watching television. Kenna was due back later than sooner, so they imagined.

Unexpectedly, they heard the key in the door. Flabbergasted, they ejected themselves from the sofa like toast from a toaster. However, Kenna had caught them off guard and they couldn't scramble apart quickly enough.

The two attempted to separate and Kenna screamed, "Don't move or I'll shoot your asses." They both froze in space with their hands up.

"Look, I can explain, p-p-please don't shoot!"

Kenna was livid and pointing the revolver dead at James. He was one clip short of getting blown away.

"It's not what it looks like, I swear!"

"Kick rocks, heifer!" Kenna shouted to Molly, James' purported lover, cocking the revolver.

"Please, just listen!" said James. L-let me tell you what hap..."

"Did I stutter? I said shut up Bobble Head before I pull this trigger!"

Kenna was nervous. She'd never handled a revolver before. She knew in her heart of hearts she wouldn't use it, but she had to let them know she was nothing to toy with.

Kenna began waving the revolver at James and Molly wildly. They were weaving and dodging with their hands up.

"What's that smell?" asked Kenna. Both of them appeared to have urinated on themselves.

"Y'all peed on yourselves?" she asked with nervous laughter.

"Yes," said James. "This wasn't part of the plan."

"I'll bet it wasn't!" said Kenna with more nervous laughter. "You thought you could get away with it and now you're busted, punk!"

"Get away with what? What are you talking about?"

"Don't play with me, Bobble Head! You must think I'm slow!" James merely stared at her, perplexed.

Kenna noting his perplexing aimed the revolver slightly away. "You really don't know what I'm talking about, do you?"

"We really don't," said Molly.

"Was I talking to you, heifer?" said Kenna, re-straightening the revolver and pointing it dead at her.

"I'm sorry!" said Molly, petrified.

"You don't remember the text you sent me about this hussy, James? It had some real nasty stuff in it about what you were going to do to her when she came over."

"Oh that. That was just a joke—wasn't it Molly?" said James, eyeing her with a smirk and clueless, with nervous laughter.

"Yeah! We were just joking," they both said, chuckling, and bucking, and bowing like buffoons.

Kenna pointed the revolver dead at both of them and cocked it. They'd gone too far and she judged she was being played.

Kenna's finger was pulling more and more on the trigger when she was suddenly tackled from behind and wrestled to the floor. She dropped the revolver that went off! Then something totally unexpected occurred!

Chapter 6

Earlier, Horwood was almost at Kenna's place. He was in a tizzy. He didn't know what was jumping off with her or what to expect. Alls he knew is that he needed to retrieve his revolver before all hell broke loose between her and James. Getting the bags switched was definitely not part of the plan.

You see, James had hired Horwood as a private investigator. He'd been concerned about his wife lately. He desired to track her whereabouts. He had a suspicion something was up between her and her kids' daddy. And he needed to know before he invested anything further into the marriage emotionally, financially, or otherwise.

If things didn't work out, he was prepared to walk away from it all and cut his losses. James had something special planned for Kenna tonight, unbeknownst to her, and Horwood was in on it. However, his revolver definitely wasn't part of it. All this had caught him off guard.

Horwood had bust through the door just in the nick of time as Kenna was seemingly about to pull the trigger. Unfortunately, the revolver went off prematurely.

***

Calvin had just been released from the hospital and turned to Claudia and said, "I'm awfully grateful you could pick me up and are taking me to my apartment. Luckily it's paid for or I'd be homeless just about now. Thank you."

"You're welcomed. I'm just thrilled you're okay."

"Listen, why don't you let me buy you dinner or something. That's the least I can do for your helping me out like this."

"That would be nice. How about tomorrow? I think you could use some rest tonight and a comfier bed than that ole hospital thing."

"You're right, I'm rather tired. Luckily this all happened before my job orientation."

"So where are you going to work now and where are you from?"

Calvin was a little ticked. While he was grateful she'd stuck it out with him, he didn't know her well enough to tell her his personal business, nor did he desire to. He couldn't get all that lip action she had on the train out his head. And even though she was reserved for the moment, he feared the yakking would resume any moment now. He decided to fabricate some stuff.

"I'll be working for a small firm in uptown Manhattan. No biggie, but it's a living."

"What will you be doing there?"

"Oh, just some customer service stuff."

"Telephone sales, eh?"

"Exactly. I'mma just do this until I'm established and can get something better." Then Calvin decided to go out on a limb and ask her about herself. "So where are you from and what do you do, may I ask?"

"I told you about all that stuff on the train—remember? Oh, I guess not, seeing what you've been through and all these past few days. Well, let met recap for you."

Oh no!

Calvin's fears resurfaced as Claudia went on and on about herself. yakkety-yak. And just think, he had to put up with this for one more night tomorrow. Her lips were yakking a thousand miles a minute. All he imagined were her bright red lips swelling and multiplying a gazillion times over. She went on and on and on and on....

By the time Claudia had said a gazillion mouthfuls, they'd reached the hotel. Calvin refrained from bolting out the vehicle. Cleary, he didn't want to hurt her feelings. After all, what would he have done without her support these couple of days?

As Claudia was driving off, Calvin said, "See you tomorrow. We can have dinner here, okay?"

"Sure, that's perfect. See you around seven?"

"Sure."

Calvin who had phoned his employer while hospitalized, entered the hotel and approached the desk. His employer had in turn called and explained his situation to the concierge staff.

"Hello Mr. Calvin, said the desk clerk. Good to see you're okay. Call if you need anything."

The clerk returned Calvin's identification to him and handed him his hotel key. Calvin road the elevator to his floor, let himself in, and sighed. "Only one more day with Ms. Motor-Mouth and she's gone for good! Once I leave here, it's good-BYE Ms. Motor-Mouth." Next he motioned to the bed, fell backwards on it, and crashed.

Chapter 7

Ulyssa arrived promptly at Ms. Lora's house. She'd journeyed through an expanse of highway and roads until she reached the inner city. She perceived it as afflicted with overcrowded buses, unkempt dwellings, pollution, littered streets, and undesirables.

Ulyssa cringed from her isolated surroundings. She was paranoid and feared for her safety. She grasped the door knob and exclaimed, "Eeeewl! Looks creepy and filthy."

Ulyssa rang the doorbell and waited for a response. Felix opened the door and she was instantly disgusted by him, recalling his remark about her panties. Felix attempted to appear warm and friendly.

"Look, let's cut to the chase, Felix. I don't have time for this. I need to get back home. I don't like it here."

"Shsssh! Don't say that so loudly. Ms. Lora might get offended. Jeez, she's your mother for Pete's sake."

"Okay, I'll lower my voice and change my tone, but I'll have to see those pictures first before I can make that determination. And here's your stinking bag!" Kenna handed over the carry-on to Felix. "Aren't you even going to invite me in?"

"Oh, excuse my manners. Come in."

Ulyssa scanned the house mortified. It was filthy and shabby. Several little critters skittered across the floor! "Oh my goodness, what's that?!" screamed Ulyssa.

"You mean you haven't seen roaches before? They won't harm you unless you let them get in your food. They're diseased you know," Felix said, snickering.

"Well, if Ms. Lora turns out to be my mother for real, I certainly wouldn't leave her here to live. I'd definitely take her home with me and sell this shack."

"I would hope so. A good daughter would anyway."

"Okay that's enough about that. Where is Ms. Lora and where are the pictures?"

Ms. Lora is in the kitchen and I'll take you there in a minute. There's your bag over there. Just have a seat here and you can look over Ms. Lora's pictures of yourself in her bag. Your name is on the back of them. I'm going to check on Ms. Lora."

Ulyssa sat with her back to Felix. Felix hadn't left just yet. While she was rattling through Ms. Lora's bag, he was nearby, licking his lips, and conjuring up nasty erotic thoughts about her. He had a wanton menacing expression on his face, when she abruptly turned her chair around and caught him off-guard.

When Ulyssa peeped Felix's serpentine expression, she froze. She was frightened out of her wits. She was about to stand when he shoved her down by her shoulders. There was a struggle. She'd toppled out of the chair and he was all over her. He had his crusty lips pressed against hers and her arms pinned.

Ulyssa kicked him in the nuts and he curled over. She tried to run, but Felix managed to snare her ankle with a one-hand firm grip while he continued to massage his crotch with the other. She cried out Ms. Lora's name and received no answer. He pulled her back down and climbed atop her.

"Now you've done it! I'm about to tear that up, he said, feasting on her crotch. She fought and fought and fought and he grew tired of her resistance, which made him antsy and aggravated; and he decided it wasn't worth the struggle. Thus he reached for a lamp, while holding her down as best he could, and clobbered her upside her head with it. Ulyssa was knocked out cold! Tears of blood dripped from her hairline.

Felix drug Ulyssa's limp body into the kitchen. He hoisted her up into a chair beside Ms. Lora who was bound and gagged and writhing, squirming, and whimpering. He bound and gagged Ulyssa's limp body in her chair and propped it against Ms. Lora's chair. Ulyssa remained unconscious.

Felix managed to abscond with Ulyssa's purse, carry-on, house and car keys, and everything of value in Ms. Lora's house. He planned with her vehicle to drive to her place, ransack her apartment, and swipe everything of value he could stuff into it and get outta Dodge. If only he knew.

***

The revolver went off! SURPRISE! HAPPY BIRTHDAY! At least two dozen people or so flooded from the kitchen.

Molly, had long ago flown the coup as soon as she was freed, her foot grazed from the gunshot. James merely froze with pee stains on his pants, and with a Cheshire Cat smile said, "Surprise, honey!"

Kenna froze with her mouth gaped and hands holding her face. She was speechless. She stared at her husband with tears of joy flowing. She then gazed at Horwood, who was grinning from ear-to-ear, ecstatic that things had worked out okay.

Kenna finally was able to say, "You mean you did all this for me? You planned this? You, too? DAMN! Is that you? You're that man from the bus! You clean up nicely Daddycito…haaay! Wait, what the hell are you doing here?"

"I'll explain it to you later," said Horwood.

"Okay," said Kenna, who couldn't seem to keep her eyes off him.

"Okay, okay, enough about all that. I gotta change out of these pissy clothes. I'll be right back, babe," said James, apparently intimidated by his wife's newfound attention to Horwood.

"Okay. I'm sorry I didn't believe you, baby."

"It's okay; you're forgiven, I'll live." And Kenna blew several kisses at her husband.

Thereafter all the guests gathered around. Earlier James had told them he'd signal for them to come out and spring the surprise on Kenna. Nate, his mother, and kids had rushed to Kenna's house as soon as she left theirs. They'd arrived not too long ago and comingled with the other guests.

Apparently, when the guests heard the gunshot, it was presumed that was the signal to appear. Whatever the case, things seemed to work out well in the end, so Kenna imagined.

****

Chapter 8

Ulyssa finally reached consciousness. She choked behind her gag and attempted to squirm out of the thin rope holding her wrists. Ms. Lora had dozed off a bit. It seemed like hours had passed.

Ulyssa eyed the kitchen frantically. It was filthy and she'd spotted about a half- dozen critters. "Ugh" she muttered under her mouth gag.

Ulyssa realized her feet were free and she hobbled over to the utensil drawer. "Ugh!" she cried. There they we're again and she fumbled around them for a knife. She hopped back over beside Ms. Lora.

"Ms. Lora, wake up! I need your help!"

Ms. Lora stirred, dazed and woozy. "Wh-what happened?!"

"Felix attacked us and probably robbed us blind. I need you to take this knife and cut me loose."

Ms. Lora obliged with shaky hands but nonetheless managed to cut through the thin rope. After they were both freed, they frantically scurried to the living room where Ulyssa's hunch was confirmed.

"He took my cell phone and purse, as suspected, so we can't call the police. I'm sure he…"

"Yes we can. I have a phone," offered Ms. Lora.

"Where?!"

"Underneath this airbed, I hope."

"Good! We'll call the cops first and then you're coming with me. Pack your stuff. You shouldn't stay here any longer. It's just not safe or sanitary here."

"But this is my home. I can't just leave it."

"Yes you can. I'll help you sell your property."

Ulyssa retrieved the phone and informed the cops. "The cops should be here soon," she assured Ms. Lora. "They'll take us to my place. And the joke's on Felix. Cars ain't what they used to be. Ha-ha!"

Ulyssa had maxed out all her credit cards. Most of the other stuff in her purse was makeup and a measly ten bucks. Her cell phone was not a concern. All her stuff was pass-worded and she could simply report the phone stolen, except it served an essential purpose for now.

***

Hold up, wait a minute! Kenna abruptly sat up in the bed beside her husband late nighttime after her birthday party. "Somethin' ain't right!" she whispered.

Kenna reflected back to the train ride. She and James had had a spat before she left and he'd refused to accompany her to her family reunion. Kenna had felt humiliated and unsupported and refused to talk to him. So she'd set her phone on airplane mode to curtail his phone calls and texts.

Three days had surpassed when she'd finally decided to check her texts and switch the mode off; that meant all of them were at least three days old.

Kenna surmised, if he was trying to rush her home, he wouldn't have done it three days ahead. There was only one way to find out.

Kenna laid back down and stared at her own cell phone lying on the nightstand. Should or shouldn't I? she thought. Do prying eyes really want to know?

Kenna stared at James fast asleep. He'd worn her out tonight with guilt-sex, perhaps. She felt equally content and loved. That reunion stuff had flown out the window with her orgasms.

Kenna turned, reached for her phone, snatched her hand back, reached again, snatched it back. This scenario played over and over and over again until she mustered the courage to read the text details. Her expression said it all—or perhaps not.

Chapter 9

Ulyssa and Ms. Lora waited for the police. Ulyssa was in a chair fixated on the critters and cringing. Ms. Lora was busy spraying galore betwixt nodding off here and there. They cracked a smile at each other intermittently and didn't utter a word initially.

Ulyssa was the first to speak up. "Felix said you had baby photos that looked like me in your carry-on."

"What are you talking about? What photos?"

"He said before he returned your carry-on, he'd riffled through it and seen the photos. Can I see them?"

"What photos? He never had my bag. My bag was by the closet, unless he went in there."

"Are you sure? He said he had your bag and you had mine."

"I never had your bag. I checked the luggage tag.

"I think you did. How else would he have known how to reach you?"

"Oh, yeah, yeah," you're right. Maybe I didn't read the tag right. I didn't have my glasses on at the time."

"Oh, so you're not possibly my mother? How long have you lived here?"

"Why are you asking me these questions? Don't you know who your mother is?"

"I'm adopted. My adoptive mom and dad died some time ago. They were kind of old when they adopted me. I have been looking for my birth mom for some time. How about you? You got any kids?"

Ms. Lora gulped. Her eyes saddened. This subject appeared to be a sore spot for her, however she mustered the courage to talk about it anyway.

"Yes, I have a daughter I put up for adoption, about your age," she began. "Her no-good father left me in the lurch and I found myself homeless and devastated. I feigned illness and wound up in the hospital.

Social Services approached me at my bedside and helped me put her up for adoption. I was so sad, I wound up in several psychiatric wards for depression. I'm still depressed. Never had any positive relationships with men. Never married. You see how I live."

"I'm so sorry, Ms. Lora. Well you won't have to worry about this anymore. Like I said, I have plenty of room at my place. I'm not attached to anyone. And as I said earlier, I can help you sell this place. You've got your Social Security—right?"

"Yes, but it's very little. I only worked a few odd jobs here and there as a cook. One thing I can say, I'm a superb cook and you can probably use one since you travel so much. And it would free me from feeling like I'm freeloading on you."

"Wow, that's a nice gesture but don't worry about it. I cook too, and I have many extensive furloughs and prepare large meals and freeze them in between. But you could help, if it makes you feel better. But mostly I want you to get on with your life and be happy. We'll do fun stuff, and frankly, I could use a mother figure."

Ms. Lora smiled seemingly for the first time. Ulyssa had made her day, so it seemed. "Oh, my two thousand dollars my cousin gave me! That was under the mattress too. Can you check it for me? I'm too tired to bend over and look."

"Sure." Ulyssa lifted the airbed and found her money sandwiched between a paper towel this time tucked away at the back end of the airbed. She supposed she didn't want to get the roaches all over it. She handled it very delicately. Eeeewl! she said to herself, and handed it over to Ms. Lora.

"Oh thank God Felix didn't see this!"

"Yes, thank God!"

"May I ask what your daughter's name was, if you don't mind?"

"Ulyssa."

Ulyssa held her mouth open and gasped! Ms. Lora peeped her expression, pleased. Oh my God! thought Ulyssa. And just then, the doorbell rang; it was the police.

Ulyssa rose from her chair and answered the door. They had Felix in custody in the squad car. Ulyssa had given them a full description of him, herself, her vehicle, belongings, Miss Lora, and her house.

"Is that him?" asked the officer, pointing to the squad car at the curb.

"Yup, that's him, alright. How'd you catch him? — Oh, I see, she said, spotting her vehicle. Apparently, he never left the house! Tee-hee," said Ulyssa, chuckling. "Wait! Where did those little dings come from?"

"Apparently, he kicked the wheels, body, and the tires. Looks like he'd been trying to figure out how to start the car and became frustrated. All your stuff is still in the car. He was scurrying down the road with your purse and a gas can when we drove up. He dropped your purse and tried to run, but naturally we had him surrounded." The officer chuckled a bit.

Felix had reportedly been quite animated, kicking the vehicle tires and body, expressing sordid frustration, intermittently cradling his head on his arms on the hood and weeping. He must've hopped in and out of the vehicle a gazillion times after failed attempts of deciphering how to start it. He'd depressed several buttons, except the ignition, and still nothing had happened. nada! He'd sobbed on the steering wheel repeatedly.

After a while, he'd dumped Ulyssa's purse and discovered a measly ten bucks and her credit cards. He scurried to the nearest store attempting to use them to no avail.

Next he approached a gas station and with the ten bucks purchased a gas can and a gallon of gas. In all his hysteria, he'd surmised that the car must've been out of gas—Yeah, that's why it didn't start, he'd reasoned. Afterwards he'd headed back to the vehicle boldly carting Ulyssa's shoulder bag and gas can. He'd attempted to abscond when the police spotted him.

Ulyssa chuckled too. "Yeah, nowadays these vehicles are equipped with all kinds of technology a lot of these hustlers don't know about. He never realized he needed to press the button to get it started. Also, the vehicle has a GPS locator as well as my cell phone. And the dealership could have frozen the car and trapped him inside once he took off in it. Furthermore, all my credit cards are maxed out, so he couldn't have done anything with those."

The officer chuckled and said, "Well, we're going to need you to make a report. When you and your mom get settled, come on down to the station and make an official report. Then he leaned in and said, "You plan to get her out of this rat hole—right? It looks condemned. We almost passed it."

"Yes, Officer…? I didn't get your name," said Ulyssa, batting her eyes.

"Rowan."

"Well, Officer Rowan, I finally convinced her to leave it. You've been very helpful. We'll see you down at the station. She's coming home with me." Officer Rowan tipped his hat and smiled and headed to the squad car and drove off.

Miss Lora had gathered her bag and began to trail Ulyssa out of the house with it. "Leave that here, Miss Lora. I'll get you a new one when I get paid. In the meantime, I'll get you what you need. My real credit card is at home," she said snickering.

Ulyssa gazed at Miss Lora dubiously. What a coincidence, she thought.

"What's wrong?" asked Ms. Lora.

"Nothing. I was thinking about something."

***

Kenna tiptoed over to James' side of the bed. There lay his cell phone. She stared at it and shook her head, no, several times before she reached for it. James stirred a bit as she seized it gingerly.

Kenna headed to the adjoining restroom and squatted on the toilet seat cover. She exhaled several times then stared at the frozen screen. And with a red-manicured finger tapped it to reactivate the screen-saver. Nothing happened! She must've tried it a gazillion times. Still, nothing happened!

Dammit, it's locked! Why is it locked?! His Bobble Head ass must be hiding somethin', she thought.

It didn't matter. As far as she was concerned, that was all the evidence she needed, and it was all over with; his ass was busted!

Next, she slithered off the toilet seat, softly opened the door, noted James was still asleep, and slipped the phone back to the nightstand. She crept to her side of the bed. That instant, James shot-opened his eyes and merely stared at his cell phone.

Uh-oh!

Kenna seized her cell phone and slipped out the bedroom door, bouncing her blond-black-streaked, weaved--hair, gossamer-nightie-, juicy-booty self down the steps. She dialed a number on her cell phone and asked, "Can you come get me?"

Chapter 10

Three days ago, Horwood had been invited to James' home to assist him with Kenna's birthday plans. James had commissioned him to wear the homeless man getup.

Secretly, James felt a tad insecure about Horwood's good looks and hence felt that things could backfire on him, ergo the repulsive disguise was borne. Molly from work had agreed to assist James who'd paid them all off.

There were snacks available and at some point Molly had ventured into the kitchen to prepare them. At the same time, James had departed upstairs. He'd inadvertently left his cell phone on the dining room table.

Horwood had seen pictures of Kenna. He was instantly attracted to her. He'd fantasized about her and unbeknownst to him, for the likes of him couldn't let them go. He had something malicious brewing in his head.

It was as though the cell phone was summoning Horwood. "Read me!" James' text messages were glaring at him. He'd confided to Horwood that Kenna had threatened to place her cell phone on airport mode, thus foiling his attempts to contact her. She was angry at him for not accompanying her to her family union, thus desired not to hear nor talk to him.

Horwood ran with this and cooked up a plan. He wanted Kenna so badly, he was willing to sabotage her marriage.

Horwood peeked over at the phone and stared at it. Momentarily, guilt overtook him that was quickly supplanted by lust. He gazed around and surreptitiously sent several lewd text messages to Kenna supposedly slated for Molly. He waited until they were certified as sent with the date and time sent confirmed. And just as he proceeded to delete the messages one by one, he heard footsteps and James appeared unexpectedly. Shortly thereafter, Molly surfaced with the snacks.

Presently, Horwood is answering his phone.

"Hello? What's the matter?"

"Listen, I think James really cheated with Molly. I know you helped him with my birthday plans."

"How'd you get this number?"

"When I had your bag."

"Oh."

"So, can I come over?"

"Sure," he said dryly, attempting to conceal his excitement. "How soon can I expect you?" he said licking his lips sinisterly.

"Soon."

"You know the address?"

"Yes, but there's just one thing—I need you to send a cab so James doesn't get suspicious. He's asleep now. I'll be waiting outside." Kenna nabbed her trench coat from the hall closet. Nightie and all, she headed quietly out the door.

***

That same night after Kenna's party, Nate's mother banged on his bedroom door. "Open up!" she shouted through it. "Let me in!"

Just a minute ma, I'm not dressed. I'm putting on my robe." Next Nate sauntered to the door with the TV blasting and cracked it.

"What did I tell you about blasting that TV like that? And what is all that nasty stuff I heard? You lookin' at the devil's movies again?"

"Ma! I'm a grown-ass man."

"Yeah, sure you are. I'll know that when you man up and get your own place."

"Ma, I'm working on it. You know that."

"How? By knocking up women? That's a baby-maker not a man. Anyway, turn that mess down! And you better not have no skank up in there. I'm warning you. What kind of example are you setting for your kids?!"

"Whatever, ma!" And Nate closed the door, disrobed, and scrambled back to the bed.

"Who's she calling a skank?" said Molly, whose head emerged from beneath the covers.

"Look!" said Nate, "If you want to continue getting somma Nate, you're going to have to keep the hollering and screaming to a minimum."

"And another thing…" said his mother, busting through the door.

Uh-oh!

Chapter 11

The ridesharing service arrived to retrieve Kenna who was headed to Horwood's. She was shedding crocodile tears throughout the journey. Just as she was nearing Horwood's place far on the other side of town, her cell phone rang.

"Mommy, can you come get us?" squealed Tequila on the phone.

"What's going on? Where's daddy and grandma?"

"Daddy's here. He told me to call. He said come get us now!"

"I'm on my way somewhere, but I guess I can just have the driver swing that way. I'll be right there, baby."

"Dammit to hell!"

***

James was trailing Kenna. He was in a tizzy. Immediately after she'd left the bedroom, he'd scrambled to get dressed. He tiptoed downstairs and overheard her whispering on her phone. Next, he'd eyed her nabbing her coat from the closet only dressed in her nightie.

Instantaneously, he'd studied his phone. He couldn't figure out for the life of him what possessed Kenna to commandeer it. Luckily it was locked. Okay, maybe locking his phone wasn't cool, but he had to in order to keep her surprise a secret. He'd forgotten in all the excitement over her birthday bash to unlock it.

James searched his phone and saw nothing that scared him. He and Kenna had discussed the meaning of the texts to throw her off—except for this one. He stared at it and whispered, "Wait a minute; I never sent this one."

Next, he reflected back on when Kenna was screaming about the nasty texts he'd sent when she was wielding the revolver, and he and Molly were pretending to know all about them.

James saw that the text was dated three days ago. Kenna had threatened to put her phone on airplane mode. He knew texting her would've been futile at that point. He'd refrained from doing so until three days later. This was definitely not among his bogus texts to throw Kenna off, and belonged to someone else.

Let's see, he thought, it's from my phone and I didn't send it. Then who did? Kenna was downstairs calling somebody. Who was around my phone that day? Molly? No, she was just as clueless about the texts as far as he could tell as he was. Then who? BINGO!

Presently, James runs upstairs quickly to retrieve something and scrambles back down. By then the ridesharing service has retrieved Kenna and is pulling off. James discretely vamooses to his vehicle and begins trailing Kenna. He is livid. "That wife-stealing creep!" he exclaims.

James surmised that Horwood had sent the texts three days ago and cleverly deleted all but one. He either missed it, or was about to get caught and couldn't get to it in time.

James had Horwood's revolver that he'd inadvertently left behind during the party, which he stuffed into his glove compartment. He was on a mission of revenge against Horwood. He drove in a fitful rage.

Chapter 12

Kenna arrived at Nate's place. She was expecting to retrieve her children only. She hadn't informed Horwood she was bringing them. She was rather apprehensive and feared his reaction.

When the driver pulled up, four persons were waiting at the curbside. Kenna blew up and screamed, "Boy, what are you doing out here?!" referring to Nate. "And where does this heifer think she's going? You two don't think you're getting in here too, do you?" said Kenna, pointing to the vehicle.

"Look, all you've got to do is drop us off. But you've got to take the kids with you, though, because mama kicked me out."

Kenna was boiling and animated and demanded the kids to get in the vehicle first. Then she turned to Nate and Molly, cussed them out, and offered to drop them off for the sake of peace after she made her pit stop.

"I can't take more than four at a time, ma'am," explained the driver.

Next, they hopped in the vehicle, which quickly sped off. Molly stood at the curbside livid and waving good-bye.

All along, James had been parked nearby peeking the whole scenario. His entire mood had changed. He knew his baby, Kenna well. He was already accustomed to the drama. He knew the score. His sides were splitting. He knew what Horwood was in for. "I'm gonna get my baby back!" he jingled.

Kenna arrived at Horwood's with her two kids and Nate. They let themselves out the vehicle and the driver pulled off cheesing big time. Horwood opened the door flabbergasted. And just then, his cell phone alarmed letting him know how much his credit card bill was from the ride over. Eeeghast!

Kenna pushed past the door and the kids went berserk. They were all over the place oohing and ahing and manhandling all Horwood's prized possessions. "You got anything to eat?" inquired Nate.

"I'm sorry," said Kenna. "I planned to come alone but all this unexpected stuff came up. Can you forgive me?"

Seconds later, Horwood was dialing the ridesharing service as they were all waiting outside his place. Kenna's phone was jumping off the hook for some reason.

James had continued trailing them closely. Seeing all the drama had him cracking up. He was in high spirits and performing karaoke with the radio. In his hysteria and joyful anticipation of his wife's return, he was inattentive to the road. His car began swerving and he lost control. His eyes gapped open.

Uh-oh!

Kenna rushed to the hospital. She was shedding crocodile tears along the way. The driver arrived and dropped the five of them off.

Upon arrival to the desk, Kenna was given her husband's room number and instructions on how to get there. Kenna so delirious, failed to listen.

When Kenna arrived to the room and peeped her husband's mummified body, and his upper extremities trapezed in midair, she fell to the floor with crying spells, "Oh Lawd, help him Jesus!" Next, she rushed to his bedside and wept on his belly.

'Squeezit,' 'Squeezit,' 'Squeezit,' sounded the wheelchair, heading toward the elevator. A patient was being pushed by the nurse. They passed by the room of the badly mangled patient.

"STOP!" the wheelchair-bound man ordered the nurse, after spotting a blond-black-weaved- head woman with her face buried in the patient's lap. The patient was animated and gesturing about in a frenzy. "Bring me in closer!" he ordered the nurse furiously who acquiesced.

"Kenna?!" James boomed angrily.

"James?!" Kenna screamed, startled and jerking her head up and toward his direction.

"You're leaving me for him?!" squealed James.

Chapter 13

The next day, Claudia arrived promptly at the hotel at seven. She was all spruced up and dressed to the nines. She wore a black slinky evening dress with red pumps, her usual red lipstick, and a set of pearls. She was looking forward to the evening.

"Hello, Ms. Claudia," said the desk clerk.

"Hey!"

"Mr. Calvin told us to expect you, he said, lewd-eyed.

"Thank you," she said, winking at him. Next she headed for the elevator to Calvin's room, back-glancing at the desk clerk all wanton-eyed.

Claudia had more tricks than a silly rabbit. She had the same little carry-on with her, except this one was clearly hers. She had all sorts of goodies in it. Calvin was clueless about what he was in for.

While Calvin found Claudia remotely attractive, it was her mouth that'd more overly turned him off. If it wasn't' for that, he would definitely do her, he thought. She wasn't half bad. If only he knew.

So when Claudia arrived to the room and knocked, and Calvin opened the door, she blew him away with her getup, which was actually enticing to him this time. He hoped she wouldn't ruin the evening with her motor mouth. We'll see, he thought.

Calvin had already ordered room service. He'd asked Claudia what she wanted when he was able to get a word in edgewise on the drive home from the hospital.

Calvin stood there speechless with the door opened. Claudia smiled at him. "Aren't you going to invite me in?" She peeked around him into the room then back at him. "Ah, I see you're ready for me."

"Yes, that's room service over there. I ordered just what you like."

"I wasn't talking about the room service," she said bullseyeing his crotch.

Calvin scrambled to cover himself up, somewhat embarrassed. "Oh," he said, and stepped aside and allowed her entry.

"Lovely place you got here. Small, but quaint, clean, neat, suitable for you I suppose?"

"Sure, It'll do for now. How about a cocktail before dinner?"

"Sounds like a plan. Whatcha got?"

"Merlot okay?"

"Perfect. Let me retrieve the glasses over there and you can pop the cork."

Claudia provocatively sauntered to the kitchenette area and retrieved the wine glasses. Calvin got an eyeful. "So far, so good," he whispered to himself.

They settled at the table and shared wine and small-talk. I suppose Claudia wasn't feeling very chatty tonight. Sexual innuendo and erotic body language and foreplay seemingly took precedence. She sipped from her glass seductively, swirling her tongue around the top of the glass and making soft suctioning noises. She consumed her meal likewise. Calvin's meal was hardly touched, so fully aroused and bullseyeing her.

After the meal, everything got hot and heavy. They couldn't keep their hands off each other. They rolled on, kissed, sucked, and gnawed each other until they were about to burst.

Claudia pulled away from Calvin and said, "Let me slip into somethin' better."

"Agreed. I'mma pare down too."

Claudia seized her carry-on bag and hauled it to the restroom. There was something in there beyond Calvin's dreams. And that wasn't necessarily a good thing.

Calvin was ecstatic about getting with Claudia. At least he'd found a way to shut her up—well maybe not this time. He'd hoped she'd live up to her rep tonight on another tip.

Claudia was in the restroom preparing her getup. She perfumed herself up, freshened up her makeup, and reddened her lips. She donned a police uniform, attached her baton, and hoisted her revolver into its holster. She pulled out her handcuffs, turned to the mirror, and smiled. "Cops and robbers, ah, my favorite game," she said coyly.

Calvin's stiff tool was waiting to handle Claudia when she came out. Needless to say, unbeknownst to Calvin, one was waiting for him likewise.

Claudia emerged from the restroom, fully strapped in her cop getup. Calvin was waiting for her, fully unclad and laid back in the king-sized bed.

"We're going to play cops and robbers."

"But I thought you were going to strip. That's more than what you had on before."

"You're absolutely right. I'm going to strip in a minute, but I just wanted to see if this is sexy to you."

"Oh, I like it, alright. Come to me."

Claudia removed her baton and stripped down to her lacy red panties and bra. She sauntered over to the bed. It was conveniently supplied with large head-posts. Next, she and Calvin got hot and heavy.

"Can I put these handcuffs on you, baby?"

"Sure babe. Knock yourself out." Calvin said, eying her wantonly.

"I want you to do something for me before I put these on you, though. I'mma need you to cup these and do some damage, she said pointing to her breasts, and some other nasty stuff to me, and then it'll be your turn—okay?"

"Anything you need babe. I'm here for you."

Claudia ogled Calvin while removing her bra and panties. She dove into the bed, laid spread-eagle, and beaconed Calvin with a red-manicured finger.

And he dug in.

After Claudia was fully satisfied, she said, "Okay, your turn."

"Wait just a minute. Let me freshen up a bit," said Calvin.

Calvin did so and returned to the bed. He eagerly jumped in spread-eagle and allowed Claudia to handcuff him. Surprisingly, Claudia began redressing herself after doing so.

"What the hell are you doing? It's my turn!"

"It's your turn alright," Claudia said. Then something utterly unexpected transpired that neither of them anticipated.

Chapter 14

Ms. Lora joined an exhaustive number of visitors lined up like ducks in a row. Near the entrance, there were lockers available for rent to deposit all her belongings in. She retained her ID for entry. Cell phones were not permitted on the premises past these perimeters.

Ms. Lora panicked! She'd forgotten her cell phone. Where was it? Did I leave it at home in the room? Did I lock my door? she thought. In the next instant, she decided it wasn't worth the stress and dropped it.

After being sniffed by a police dog, Ms. Lora was confronted by a corrections officer. She was asked to empty her pockets and to undergo a security check comparable to LaGuardia Airport's, of not standing more than so many feet away, removing her shoes, then proceeding through a metal detector.

Finally, after enduring the rigmarole of the prison procedure, Ms. Lora was led to a room filled with tables and plastic chairs. She was instructed on which side of the table to sit. She was edgy until Felix was ushered out in a jumpsuit and plastic sandals.

Ms. Lora cracked a smile and asked, "So what's it like in here?"

"What's it to you? Hey, if you want to trade places with me, I'm sure that can be arranged once I get out of here."

"Well how long you got?"

"Not long, since I didn't get very far nor actually stole anything of major value. So, how's Ulyssa treating you? Is she on to us?"

"Obviously not, or she would've kicked my ass out by now—you think?"

"Okay, smart-ass, I didn't ask you all that."

"You think I don't know you tried to ditch me you Jack-ass? The mouth gag was a nice touch, but you must think I'm slow. I'm an old broad that's been there and done that."

You don't have to tell me, you old crone, Felix thought. "Well, good for you. Look I'm sorry about all this. Maybe we can give it another shot."

"Nice try! Be strong. See you in a couple of weeks," Ms. Lora sneered, as the guard arrived and returned her card, this signaling the end of her visit. Felix nodded goodbye as he was being returned to his cell. It would be the last time Ms. Lora laid eyes on him.

***

"Well, what are you waiting for?" It's your turn to do me, said Calvin.

"It's my turn, alright," said Claudia, fully-clothed in her police getup with her baton and revolver

"Why did you get dressed again? I wanted to feel you up."

Claudia approached the bed with her revolver drawn with one hand and keyed open the handcuffs with the other. "Get dressed, punk! You're under arrest!"

"For what? You mean that's a real gun and uniform? You're really a cop?"

"Wanna see?" And she shot a hole in the floor.

"Who's gonna pay for that?!" Calvin screamed, scurrying to get dressed. "You'll get me fired!"

"That's the least of your worries, mon."

And just like that, the walls seemingly closed in around Calvin and he couldn't have heard a bull horn if he tried. The accident must have jarred his ear drums somehow, causing sudden unexpected hearing loss. Claudia's mouth was moving a mile a minute and yakking up a storm. Alls he envisioned was her blood-red painted lips multiplying as she yakked. And worse yet—he couldn't even hear himself; it was as though he was in a vacuum. And unbeknownst to him, his speech was slurred, thus Claudia was oblivious to his pleas. Alas, his prayers had been answered!

Claudia was talking a mile a minute as she explained to Calvin about his nonpayment of child support and was reading his Miranda rights, to which he nodded and responded with slurred speech. She took his head-nodding as his affirmative understanding of his rights. Calvin became limp and delusional. She re-cuffed him roughly behind his back, shoved him into the hallway, and into the elevator.

Claudia and Calvin made it to the lobby. The police were waiting on him outside in their squad car as Claudia led Calvin out. He was yakking a mile a minute, yakkety-yakkety-yakkety-yak with slurred speech, attempting to explain his situation. All his apprehenders could envision was a set of his lips multiplying and yakking up a storm. Would he shut up, already? they thought. No one had a clue about his hearing loss.

The desk clerk, Alexander, who'd gotten an eyeful, stared at Claudia and winked. Claudia winked back and smiled.

Later on that evening, a couple lay in a luxurious king-sized bed under 1000 thread count sheets Claudia had ordered from room service on the hotel tab. They felt satisfied after a romp in the hay following room service consisting of a lavish meal of lobster, steak, caviar, tiramisu, champagne, and the works.

"So, when are you going to let his employers know what happened?" asked Alexander, the desk clerk.

"Me? That's not my responsibility. They'll find out at the end of the month when they get this big-ass bill and eviction papers. They'll be clueless about what happened to him."

"Well, what if they come out and investigate?"

"Well, who's going to tell them?" asked Claudia, gingerly massaging Alexander's genitals.

He cast her a sleazy Cheshire Cat smile.

Chapter 15

Ms. Lora struggled out of the cab with the assistance of the driver. Before she arrived, she was reflecting on her trip regarding Cousin Eloise's will.

Ms. Lora's family decided to treat her to her favorite restaurant, Lambert's Café, before her return home. They traveled to magnificent Foley Alabama eight miles north of Gulf Shores. This cafe was located beside a factory outlet mall and a hub of places to visit. One of the greatest benefits was being only eight miles away from the beach. The service was impeccable and the food arrived in big-ass portions. A cup of coffee was no less than about a half-quart a cup, so it seemed.

Besides the big-ass portioned hearty meals the café was set apart from others. It had a unique way of serving dinner rolls. You see, in 1976, Norman Lambert, son of the Founders and Owners, Earl and Agnes Lambert, threw their first roll, henceforth known for its throwed rolls. Initially, the establishment had become so busy that one day a customer requested that Norman Lambert "throw the damn thing" to him, so frustrated at the chance of not getting his roll. Hence the theme: 'Home of Throwed Rolls' was borne.

Ms. Lora was enjoying her time with her family perusing the menu when suddenly a roll came crashing upside her head. The waiter rushed over apologizing saying, "I'm so sorry. Let me clean that up for you." Ms. Lora received an eyeful of him and cheesed big time.

The waiter eyed Ms. Lora and thought, I know that ole goat ain't trying to flirt with me, ole nasty dog. And Ms. Lora seemingly thought she read his mind but in fact misread him and thought, I know he ain't trying to hit on me, ole nasty dog. He is kinda cute, though, she thought.

"Look, what can I do to make this up to you?" asked the waiter.

"A cup of coffee will do," said Ms. Lora cheesing again.

The family had arrived rather late to the restaurant. There were children among them, thus they'd made a gazillion toilet stops along the way. Ms. Lora decided to take a toilet break and en route, nearly knocked the waiter over. She was perky from the big-ass cup of coffee she'd just had along with the big-ass glasses of coke. She would be wired from this over the next day or so. If only she knew.

Ms. Lora zoomed from the restroom and beckoned the waiter over with a red-manicured finger and ignited a little small-talk "What's your name, by the way?"

"Felix. What's yours?" he asked, not that he cared.

"Ms. Lora."

Then Felix cooked up a plan, seeing how she was interested in him and all. She appeared somewhat well to do to him, all jazzy and all. He desired to feel her out.

"Look, I got a few weeks' vacation coming. How about we hang out? I'm off work in a few minutes."

"Well, I'm about to return home. My flight leaves tomorrow evening. I'm staying with relatives at the moment. Foley is quite a distance from their home. How would I get back?"

"Don't worry, I'll see to that. In the meantime, we can take a stroll on the beach and feel each other out to see if we have a connection."

"Sounds like a plan to me. I'll go let my family know. I'll just tell them you're an old friend, that way they won't get worried or suspicious."

"Good lookin' out. See you in the front then in a few?"

"Sure."

Ms. Lora was ecstatic. She was a bit hot for Felix. It'd been ages since she'd been in the company of a man. She was hoping sparks would fly.

Felix was ecstatic. I hope the ole broad is loaded. Then maybe we can find ourselves a victim and double the Jackpot. Then I can ditch the ole ball and chain and get me some pretty young thang, he thought snickering sinisterly.

The couple headed for the beach in Felix's old jalopy and they strolled along conversing and eventually holding hands. Felix, for sure, would discover a way to swindle the inheritance Ms. Lora foolishly revealed to him and more. And in order to convince her to take him back home with her to see what she had going that he could shyster her out of, he decided to feign a love interest in her. Thus they became intimate that night.

Felix simply closed his eyes, darkened the hotel room, and handled Ms. Lora as little as possible, repulsed by her saddle bags, though he was not shy of them himself.

That next early evening, they were both passengers aboard the same aircraft. However, unbeknownst to Ms. Lora, Felix secured a round trip ticket with the intention of running off with her loot and never laying eyes on her again. Before they departed the plane, Felix texted Ms. Lora that it was best they arrive at her home separately. However, the switched carry-ons was not part of the plan.

Currently, Ms. Lora had made it through the posh lobby to the elevator. She cruised to the twelfth floor of the high-rise apartment building. And as she was inserting her key into the door, Ulyssa snatched it open, appearing disheveled.

"Where have you been?!" I've been worried sick and trying to reach you all day. Why didn't you answer your cell phone?"

"Sorry, Hun; I lost it."

Ulyssa inhaled and responded calmly, "Oh. Then we'll just have to get you a new one."

"Thank you, baby. You're such a good daughter."

Ms. Lora retreated to her bedroom and closed and locked the door. She carefully removed her silver wig and the tiny pillow she'd concocted to imitate her dowager's hump. She removed the saggy pillows from her chest, the old-lady clothing, and hopped energetically into her bed. She appeared to be at least ten years younger. She smiled and thought, I'm glad to get rid of that dead weight, referring to Felix. The sex was good though, ole nasty dog. She smiled and curled under the covers and crashed.

Ulyssa returned to her bedroom and locked the door.

"Well, so what'd she say?" asked a baritone voice. "Let me guess--she lost it."

"Yup!"

"Then what'd you say, baby?"

"That I'd buy her a new one of course."

"And naturally she didn't argue with you."

"You know it."

"She had no idea I could hear her phone buzzing through the door. She didn't even have sense enough to lock it either. There were all kind of pictures of she and Felix and them texting each other. Strange, though, he didn't mention any baby photos. He must've cooked that one up himself as part of his plan to ditch her. It appears she and he were lovers. And see how she looks in these pictures?"

"So much for the Hunchback of Michigan, huh?" he chuckled.

"I think throwing her under the bus through her for a loop, though. She was probably caught off guard when he clobbered her too. Serves both of them right!" Ulyssa concluded and chuckled.

Ulyssa knew back at Ms. Lora's house her story was bogus. After all, she was not adopted. She'd only said that to them both to test their truths.

When Ms. Lora admitted not having the photos, Ulyssa hadn't put two and two together that she was in cahoots with Felix, given she was tied up and he'd robbed and abandoned them both. She'd merely felt sorry for Ms. Lora, hence decided to be a good Samaritan and house her until she could do better.

Ulyssa had taken pictures of the pictures in Ms. Lora's phone as evidence in case she tried to deny it. She showed these to her lover.

"Oh my; definitely not the old biddy she purports to be. So lemme get this straight; You had his bag and he had yours, but pretended he had Ms. Lora's knowing full well he was in cahoots with her. Then she almost blew her cover when she blurted out to you she had her own bag, then caught herself and recovered—right? And to make matters worse, he turned around and duped her."

"Exactly. But I hadn't put two and two together at the time, being so discombobulated and all."

"Understandable. So what do you want to have happen here? Do you want me to help you put her out now?"

"Hecky naw! And let her spoil my fun with you? Since she's not onto us, she's not going anywhere for now. We'll do it tomorrow."

"Then get your little sexy romp back in this sac."

"Or else what?"

"I'll have to arrest you."

"Yes Officer Rowan."

And Ulyssa charged to the bed, hopping in with the heels of her hands squeezed together, and cheesing.

The next day, Ms. Lora was escorted from Ulyssa's place by Officer Rowan with the assistance of a few of his fellow officers he'd enlisted. They drove her back to her home.

Hours later, Ms. Lora lay in her bed resuming from her nap. SPLAT! SPLAT! About half a dozen little critters skittered across the floor. Squish! Squish! Went the insecticide spray nozzle.

THE END

Printed in the United States
By Bookmasters